Aunt Ippy's MUSEUM OF JUNK

BY RODNEY A. GREENBLAT

HarperCollins*Publishers*

Library of Congress Cataloging-in-Publication Data
Greenblat, Rodney Alan, date
  Aunt Ippy's museum of junk/by Rodney Alan Greenblat.
     p.   cm.
  Summary: A brother and sister visit their ecology-minded Aunt Ippy
and her world-famous Museum of Junk.
  ISBN 0-06-022511-4. — ISBN 0-06-022512-2 (lib. bdg.)
  [1. Junk—Fiction. 2. Recycling (Waste)—Fiction. 3. Aunts—
Fiction.] I. Title.
PZ7.G8277Au 1991   90-44939
[E]—dc20   CIP
                                             AC

1 2 3 4 5 6 7 8 9 10
First Edition

Dedicated to my favorite planet,

Earth

There is nobody quite like our Aunt Ippy.

Aunt Ippy gives us the biggest hugs.

Aunt Ippy bakes the best batch of chocolate chip cookies.

Aunt Ippy can fix anything.

Aunt Ippy never throws anything away.
She uses things over and over again.

She has built a raft out of plastic milk jugs.

Her car runs on old cooking oil.

She has created a tower of two-hundred toilet paper tubes.

Don't even *look* in her garage.

Aunt Ippy calls this "Waste Management."

When she finally finds something she can't use for anything else,
she puts it into her museum.

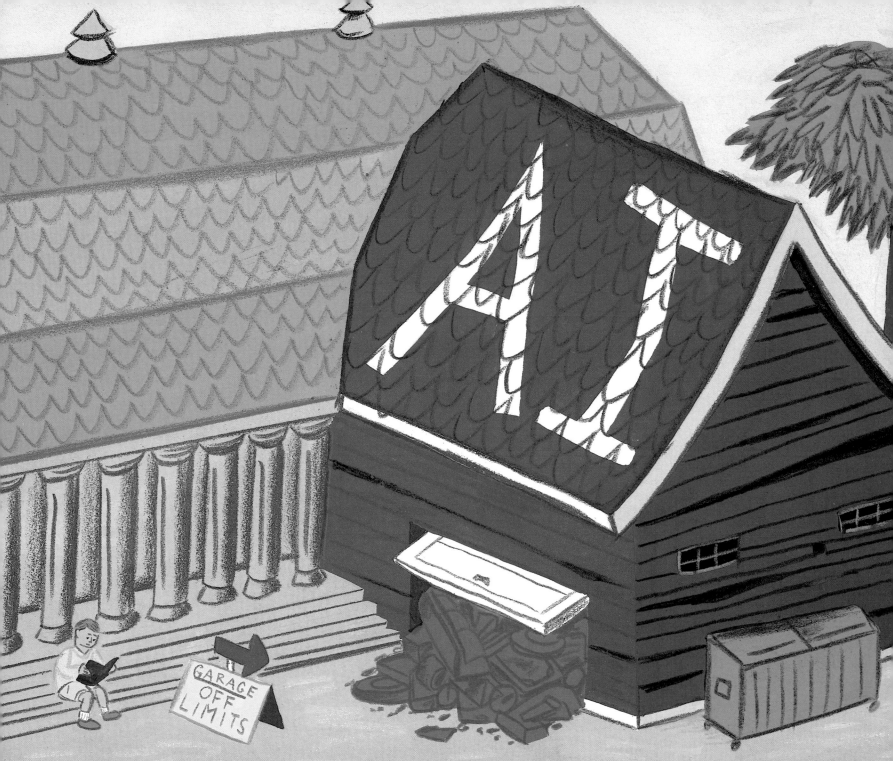

People come from near and far to visit Aunt Ippy's Museum of Junk.

This busy Sunday a man named Mr. McCorkle has come to see a Roto-Spinner, a thing he read about in *Dump Hunt* magazine.

Aunt Ippy says she knows where everything is,
but she isn't sure about the Roto-Spinner.
She asks us if we will help her find it.

We walk into the museum through the Rainbow of Shoe Boxes,
and then into the Grand Parlor of Scraps.

We are greeted by Muffler Head,
a friendly robot made of old car parts.
He tells us to look for the Roto-Spinner
in Room Ten, the Gallery of Absurd Bulk.

On the way, Aunt Ippy shows us some of her most exciting displays.

We even go through the Tunnel of Tires
and get all dirty.

In the Gallery of Absurd Bulk we see quite a bit of stuff, but no Roto-Spinner.

The Chamber of Odds and Ends is full of stuff
we have never even heard of, *but no Roto-Spinner.*

Aunt Ippy looks grim.

"It must be in the garage!" she says.

The garage is the most gigantic, fantastic, overwhelming pile of junk ever. This is where Aunt Ippy puts everything before it gets into the museum.

Mr. McCorkle looks scared.

Suddenly, from a cardboard box,
Aunt Ippy pulls out a curious-looking device.

ROTOSPIN

"This is a Roto-Spinner!" declares Aunt Ippy.

We all dance and cheer!

"But what does it do?" we all ask.

When our parents come to pick us up,
Aunt Ippy gives each of us a funny thing.
We're starting our own Museum of Junk at home!